The story of Joseph appears in the Bible in the Book of Genesis, chapters 37-47.

Joseph's Special Coat

Colin and Sheila Smithson

Zondervan Publishing House
Grand Rapids, Michigan

Joseph, the son of Jacob was a really good son. He never did anything wrong! He was so good that it annoyed his brothers.

Also there was that coat! Jacob had given Joseph a very fine coat. Joseph could not work when he wore it. This made his brothers angrier still!

Another thing that annoyed his brothers was that Joseph told them that God had shown him the meaning of dreams.

One dream he had was that one day all his family would bow down to him.

"What nonsense!"

"Joseph is a bighead!"

The brothers plotted to put an end to Joseph.

First they threw him down a well, but rather than kill him they sold him to Arab merchants who were on their way to Egypt.

The brothers now had to face their father, Jacob. They did not want him to search for Joseph and bring him back. As far as the family was concerned – Joseph was dead!

So they took Joseph's special coat and smeared it with blood. They would tell Jacob that a lion had dragged Joseph away.

Many years passed by but Joseph's troubles were not over. He was put into prison in Egypt even though he was not guilty! One day, however, the Pharaoh, the king of Egypt, sent for him.

The king had had two upsetting dreams that even his court magicians could not understand. He needed help.

Someone who had heard Joseph explaining the meaning of dreams while in prison told Pharaoh.

So Joseph was dragged out of prison and ordered to tell Pharaoh about his dreams.

"I cannot tell you" said Joseph. "But God can."

Joseph prayed and God told Joseph the meaning of Pharaoh's dreams.

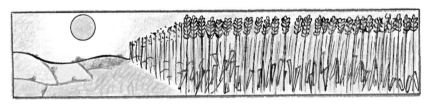

"God has given you a warning. There will be a famine; the crops will not grow for seven years.

"But first there will be seven years of great harvests.

"You must build storehouses to keep the extra grain each good year to eat in the seven bad years."

Pharaoh believed Joseph and rewarded him by making him his second in command.

And sure enough the drought came exactly seven years later. It not only attacked Egypt, but also Canaan — the home of Joseph's family. They were running out of food.

But everyone in Canaan knew there were stores of grain in Egypt. So Joseph's brothers set off for Egypt to buy food.

When they arrived in Egypt, they went to the palace to beg for food. And guess who they had to bow down before? Joseph! But they did not recognize him dressed like an Egyptian.

Joseph knew them at once.

He made a plan – to bring all his family to safety in Egypt, and also to teach his brothers a lesson.

"You are spies," Joseph suddenly said, "here to see how strong we are!"

The brothers were terrified.

"Not us," they begged.

"We have a young brother, Benjamin, and an old father at home. They are both starving".

"Bring this 'Benjamin' to me," demanded Joseph.

The brothers rushed home, taking corn with them, and begged Jacob to allow Benjamin to return with them.

They came back with Benjamin and Joseph gave them a great feast.

He still wanted to punish his brothers for what they had done to him so he hid one of Pharaoh's precious goblets in Benjamin's sack, and they set off home.

Joseph sent his men to search the sacks.

"I can have you killed for this!" Joseph said.

The brothers were dismayed. One minute they were free; the next, trapped.

But then Joseph showed himself to his brothers and spoke in their language.

"Do not be afraid" he said.

"God has sent me here ahead of you. He knows we will all be better off here. But Jacob must come to Egypt, too."

The family returned to Jacob and told him how Joseph was alive, not dead, and ruler of a great kingdom.

"The king, Pharaoh, is so pleased with him that he will do anything to help us move to his land. "We must sell everything and move to Egypt to be saved from the famine."

But Jacob asked God for himself.

God said "Go into Egypt. I will go with you and make you a great nation there."

And so the whole family of Israel went to live in Egypt.

God had prepared a way for them to live in safety.